King
&
King

Library of Congress Cataloging-in-Publication Data
Haan, Linda de, 1976-
  [Koning & Koning, English]
  King & King / Linda de Haan & Stern Nijland
      p. cm.
Summary: When the queen insists that the prince get married and take
over as king, the search for a suitable mate does not turn out as
expected.
  [1. Kings, queens, rulers, etc.--Fiction. 2. Princes--Fiction.
3. Homosexuality--Fiction.] I. Title: King and King. II. Nijland, Stern,
1976- III. Title.
  PZ7.H11132 Ki 2002
  [E]--dc21

                            2001005082

ISBN 978-1-58246-061-1

Printed in China

Book design by Betsy Stromberg
Typeset in DaddyOHip, Bailey Quad, Bailey Sans, and Blackadder

15 — 16

First American Edition

King
&
King

Linda de Haan & Stern Nijland

Tricycle Press

Berkeley

On the tallest mountain above the town lived a queen,
the young crown prince,
and the crown kitty.

The queen had ruled for many long years and she was tired of it.
She made up her mind that the prince would marry
and become king before
the end of the summer.

happy

Smile!

Traumhochzeit

ROMANCE

Dolce Vita

it's high time

trots

goed

Excellence

The Papermill

moo

importance

Open-air swimming pool

LOVE

Marrying!

to care for

mag he create happiness el wat willen

dream wedding

marrying

I DO IT FOR YOU

"You're getting married

and that's all there is to it."

The prince pushed a w a y his breakfast.
He couldn't eat a bite as the queen talked on...
and on...
and on.

"I don't understand you. Every prince in these parts is married. Every one of them but **you**! When I was your age, I'd been married **twice** already."

By evening, all that talking had made the prince **dizzy**.

"Very well, Mother. I'll marry. I must say, though, I've never cared much for princesses."

That night, the queen found her list of princesses and called every castle, alcazar, and palazzo near and far.

The very next morning, a crowd waited at the gates.

Princess Aria from **Austria** sang a **thunderous** opera for the prince. No sooner had she finished than she was shown the door.

Princess Dolly had flown all the way from Texas with her special magic act.

(The crown kitty

was happy

to assist.)

But the queen and the prince were

not amused.

Next came the **funny** little princess from **Greenland**.
The prince didn't hit it off with her either,

so he really didn't mind
when his page promptly
fell in love with her.

"**Boy**, those long arms will certainly come in handy when waving to the people," said the prince.

f l a s h

As fast as her elegant legs could carry her, Princess **Rahjmashputtin** from **Mumbai** stormed out of the palace.

The queen and the prince looked at one another sadly.

None of this was quite what they had expected.

"Wait!"
called the page.
"There is **one** more princess.
Ahem!
Presenting Princess Madeleine
and her brother,
Prince Lee."

At last, the prince felt a stir in his heart.

It was love at first sight.

"What a wonderful **prince!**"

"What a wonderful **prince!**"

The wedding was very special.

The queen even shed a tear or two.

The two princes are known as **King** and **King**,
the queen finally has some time for herself,

And everyone lives happily ever after.